Caramel Moon

READ ALL THE CANDY FAIRIES BOOKS!

Chocolate Dreams

Rainbow Swirl

COMING SOON:

Cool Mint

Candy Fairies

Caramel Moon

HELEN PERELMAN

ILLUSTRATED BY
ERICA-JANE WATERS

ALADDIN
NEW YORK   LONDON   TORONTO   SYDNEY

This book is a work of fiction. Any references to historical events, real people, or real locales are used fictitiously. Other names, characters, places, and incidents are the product of the author's imagination, and any resemblance to actual events or locales or persons, living or dead, is entirely coincidental.

ALADDIN

An imprint of Simon & Schuster Children's Publishing Division

1230 Avenue of the Americas, New York, NY 10020

First Aladdin paperback edition August 2010

Text copyright © 2010 by Helen Perelman

Illustrations copyright © 2010 by Erica-Jane Waters

For information about special discounts for bulk purchases, please contact Simon & Schuster Special Sales at 1-866-506-1949 or business@simonandschuster.com.

The Simon & Schuster Speakers Bureau can bring authors to your live event. For more information or to book an event contact the Simon & Schuster Speakers Bureau at 1-866-248-3049 or visit our website at www.simonspeakers.com.

Designed by Karin Paprocki

The text of this book was set in Berthold Baskerville Book.

Manufactured in the United States of America

0713 OFF

6 8 10 9 7

Library of Congress Control Number 2009029950

ISBN 978-1-4169-9456-5

ISBN 978-1-4424-0716-9 (eBook)

For Bethany Buck,
who was born under a Caramel Moon!

Contents

Caramel Moon

CHAPTER

1

Golden News

The caramel stalks on the hill glowed golden in the late afternoon sun. Melli, a Caramel Fairy, took a deep breath. She smelled the sweet, sugary scent of fresh caramel. Sitting on a branch of a chocolate oak, she gave a heavy sigh. It was nice to relax after a day's work in the fields.

From the tree she could see out to Caramel

Hills and Candy Corn Fields. This was one of her favorite spots in Sugar Valley. A gentle breeze blew her short, dark hair. The cool air reminded her that the weather was turning colder. While she was sorry that the long, sunny days of summer were over, Melli loved the change of season.

Autumn was the busiest time of year for the Caramel Fairies. Many of their candies were grown and harvested in the autumn months. And Melli's favorite was candy corn. Not only did she love the sweet treat, she loved the Caramel Moon Festival, too.

This event, the best event of the fall, was held during the evening of the full moon in the tenth month of the year. Princess Lolli, the ruling fairy princess of Candy Kingdom, officially named that moon Caramel Moon. The candy corn was at the peak of perfection at that time, and all the candy crops needed to be picked when they were ripe, so all the fairies in Sugar Valley came to help. The festival was a giant party with lots of candy corn, music, and dancing.

"Hi, Melli!" Cara called out. Cara was Melli's little sister. She flew up and sat on the branch beside Melli.

"Hey, Cara," Melli said. "How'd you find me?"

"I knew you'd be here," Cara told her. "It's almost Sun Dip and you always wait for Cocoa here."

Melli laughed. Her little sister was right. The chocolate oak at the bottom of Caramel Hill was at the edge of Chocolate Woods. The old tree was the perfect meeting spot for her and her best friend, Cocoa the Chocolate Fairy. They always flew together to see their friends at the end of the day when the sun dipped below the Frosted Mountains. Sun Dip was a time for meeting friends and sharing news of the day.

"I just heard some golden news," Cara went on. A smile spread across her face. "You'll never guess who is playing at the Caramel Moon Festival this year!" Her lavender wings fluttered so fast that she flew up off the branch.

"You found out who is playing?" Melli asked. Her dark eyes sparkled with excitement.

All year long, fairies tried to guess who would play the music at the late-night celebration. After the candy corn was picked, all the fairies celebrated by the light of the moon. Good music was a key ingredient to making the party a success.

Since this year Melli was old enough to have planted the seeds in the fields, she was even more excited about the festival.

Cara grinned at Melli. She usually didn't hear juicy information before her older sister. She wanted to savor the sweet moment of knowing something before Melli.

"Come on," Melli urged. "Please tell me! I want to know!" She grabbed Cara's hand.

"Well, it's your favorite band," Cara said. She looked as if she would burst with excitement.

Melli's mouth fell open. "The Sugar Pops are coming here?" Her purple wings began to flutter, and her heart began to beat faster. "Are you sure?"

"Sure as sugar," Cara said. "I was at Candy Castle to make a delivery and I heard the Royal Fairies talking about the Caramel Moon Festival. The Sugar Pops are really coming!"

The Sugar Pops were the most popular band in the entire kingdom. Their music was fun to dance to, and Melli knew every single song by heart. She also knew everything about Chip, Char, and Carob Pop. The three Pop brothers sang *and* played instruments. They had the sweetest songs.

"Hot caramel!" Melli exclaimed. "Wait until I tell everyone at Sun Dip!" She reached out and hugged her sister. "Thanks for telling me, Cara. This is fantastic news." Her mind was racing. "If they sing 'Yum Pop,' I will melt!"

Cara nodded. "Oh, they have to play that

song!" she exclaimed. "It's their best one." She smiled.

Melli looked toward Chocolate Woods. She kept an eye out for Cocoa. Cocoa loved the Sugar Pops too. Actually, all her friends did. And this year they would be able to stay and help harvest the crops, which meant they'd also get to see the Sugar Pops perform.

"What about me? Do you think I can watch the Sugar Pops?" Cara asked.

"I'll see if I can get you permission," Melli said. She leaned in closer to Cara and put her arm around her. She didn't want to see her sister so sad. "Maybe you can come for one or two songs."

"Thanks, Melli," Cara said. Her wings perked up a little at the possibility of seeing the band play.

Just at that moment, Cocoa flew up to the chocolate oak. "Hello, fairies!" she called out. "What's new and delicious?"

Melli and Cara both grinned.

"What?" Cocoa asked. She looked at the two sisters. "What are you up to?"

Melli's wings flapped and she floated off the branch. She couldn't contain her excitement! "Cara found out that the Sugar Pops are playing at the Caramel Moon Festival!" she burst out.

Cocoa clapped her hands. *Choc-o-rific!* she shouted. "That is the sweetest news I've heard all day!" She sat down on one of the chocolate oak's branches. "Wait until the others hear about this. And this year we'll get to stay the whole night!"

Melli nudged Cocoa. She knew that Cara was feeling sad about not being old enough to

stay for the night concert. "We're going to see if Cara can come for at least one song," she told Cocoa.

"'Yum Pop', I hope," Cara said. She held up crossed fingers.

Melli and Cocoa laughed.

"Come on," Cocoa said. "Let's head over to Sun Dip and tell the others."

"I want to go check on the candy corn crops before Sun Dip," Melli said. "All the Caramel Fairies were working near Caramel Hills today. I haven't been since yesterday. I'll meet you at Red Licorice Lake."

Melli gave quick hugs to Cara and Cocoa.

"I'll see you later," Cara called as she flew back home to Caramel Hills.

"See you soon, Cara," Cocoa said. "And, Melli, bring some of your caramel!"

"Of course!" Melli called. She still had a smile on her face as she flew toward the fields.

The Caramel Moon Festival was bound to be the most extraordinary event of the year!

Sugar Valley PRESENTS
CARAMEL MOON FESTIVAL
With Surprise Special guest band!!

2

Trouble in the Fields

Melli found herself alone in Candy Corn Fields. The early evening chill felt refreshing, and the crisp smell of the crops meant that harvest time was nearing.

As she flew through the fields, she hummed a Sugar Pops song. She imagined how fun it would be to dance to their music at midnight after all the crops were picked. There would be a stage set up at the north side of the fields. Large barrels of candy corn would line the stage, and Princess Lolli would welcome all the Candy Fairies. She was a fair and true ruler, who took good care of all the fairies in Sugar Valley. And she was also a huge fan of the Sugar Pops!

Melli wondered if she would get to meet the Pop boys. She had to at least get their autographs! She fluttered her wings just thinking of the three sweet singers.

Landing in the green fields, Melli looked around. Her wings drooped as she spun in a circle. It wasn't the color of the stalks or the shapes of the hanging candy corn that concerned her. But something was wrong. Very wrong.

She flapped her wings and flew up and down the rows. Her wings beat faster as she looked around. All the stalks were much shorter than they had been the day before. The stalks were supposed to grow taller, with candy corn dripping from the wide leaves. But at that moment it seemed to Melli that the stalks had shrunk.

How can this be? she thought. *What happened? I was just here yesterday.*

As Melli flew up and down the rows of candy corn stalks, she didn't notice the darkening sky. The sun had just slipped down past the Frosted Mountains when she heard Cocoa's voice.

"Melli!" Cocoa cried. She waved her hands, trying to get her friend's attention.

"Over here," Melli answered. She didn't look up from the stalk she was examining.

"What's the matter? You missed Sun Dip!" Cocoa said as she flew up to Melli. "Everyone was so worried."

"Something is not right here," Melli blurted out. She pointed to the stalks around them.

Melli slowly walked a few steps. She leaned in close to the stalks. The white, yellow, and orange candy corn looked all right, but something seemed off to her. "These stalks were higher yesterday," she explained to Cocoa. She flapped her wings and took off down the row.

"What do you mean?" Cocoa asked. She took flight and followed her friend. "Everything looks fine."

As Cocoa flew down the long rows, the green leaves of the stalks tickled her arms. She saw that all the stalks were filled with candy corn. "The candy corn looks delicious," she said. "Especially the ones on the far end of the field."

"You mean the ones with the chocolate tips?" Melli asked. She knew that Cocoa preferred the ones with a touch of chocolate.

"Actually," Cocoa said, "all these look ready for harvesting." She smelled the sweet scent of ripe candy corn. "This all looks good to me."

"I'm telling you, something is wrong," Melli replied. Her wings fluttered quickly as she flew down to examine another stalk. She shook her head sadly. "Caramel Moon is two days from now. What happens if the candy corn doesn't ripen in time? Or worse, if the candy corn shrinks and disappears!"

Cocoa gasped. There had never been a year without candy corn. She wasn't sure what all the fairies would do without the special autumn treat.

"How can we have a Caramel Moon Festival without candy corn?" Melli cried out.

Cocoa put her arm around her friend. "Don't be silly," she said. "The corn is always ready on the night of Caramel Moon. You worry too much." She spun around and looked at the rows of green stalks. "The fields are full, and the candy corn looks ready to harvest!" She saw that Melli was still concerned. "Has Princess Lolli been here yet? Maybe she can help."

"She hasn't been here yet," Melli said. "She said she'll be by soon to check on the crops." Melli stepped on a mound of soft brown sugar. "I don't really want her to see the fields looking

like this!" Staring down at the ground, she mumbled, "What if I did something wrong?"

"What are you talking about?" Cocoa asked. "I think you are just nervous. All this talk about the Sugar Pops coming has distracted you!"

"No," Melli said. She searched the fields for a clue. "This is strange."

"I don't know," Cocoa told her. "Maybe you just have the sugar jitters for the big day."

Melli ducked low and peered under one of the stalks. "Look!" she cried, pointing. "There's a mound of brown sugar here," she said. "And fallen candy corn on the ground over there." She crawled under a stalk and followed the trail of clues.

Cocoa came with her. Maybe Melli was right. Normally, the fields didn't look like someone—

or something—had been pulling corn off the stalks.

"The whole north part of the field is ruined!" Melli exclaimed. "Someone has been messing with the candy corn crops. And we have to find out who!"

Cocoa bent down and picked up a mashed candy corn. "Look at this," she said. "You're right, Melli. Candy corn doesn't get mashed by itself."

Melli's eyes widened. "Do you think someone is trying to ruin the Caramel Moon Festival?" she asked.

"I don't know," Cocoa admitted. "But sure as sugar, we need to find out!"

3

Candy Clues

As Melli and Cocoa picked up the fallen stalks and candy corn, their friends arrived at Candy Corn Fields.

"What's going on?" Raina asked. The Gummy Fairy looked worried as she saw her friends scurrying around the fields.

Dash, a Mint Fairy, flew above them. "Are

you picking the candy before Caramel Moon?"

"Of course they aren't," Berry said. The beautiful Fruit Fairy landed on the ground and leaned over to smell the candy corn. "Everyone knows that the candy isn't picked until midnight of the Caramel Moon."

"Someone has been messing with the crops," Melli blurted out.

"Are you sure?" Berry asked. She looked around the dark fields. "What makes you think that?"

Melli pointed to the basket of smashed candy corn and broken stalks that she and Cocoa had collected. "See?" she said. "The north side of the field was a mess. I think someone was trying to take all the candy corn."

"No one has ever stolen candy corn from the

fields," Raina said, shaking her head. Raina knew the whole history of the Candy Fairies and Candy Kingdom. She loved to read and had memorized the Fairy Code Book. "I've never heard of such a story about Candy Corn Fields."

"There's a first time for everything," Dash said as she landed on top of one of the candy corn stalks.

"Dash!" Berry scolded. She saw Melli's worried expression. She didn't want to send Melli into a sugar fit. She already looked like she was ready to have a meltdown.

"Maybe one of the other Caramel Fairies was trying to get the fields ready?" Raina offered.

"No Caramel Fairy would pick the candy before Caramel Moon," Melli said. "The Caramel Fairies were working in the south part of the fields yesterday. This must have happened overnight and no one checked on this side today." She examined the stalk next to her. "It's almost as if someone was trying to pull down the stalks." She pointed to the short stalk in front of her.

"Remember those chocolate bugs that ate away at the trees in Chocolate Woods last year?" Cocoa asked. "Maybe it's some kind of candy field bug?"

Raina shook her head. "They wouldn't be strong enough," she said. "These stalks are thick and very sturdy." She reached over and gave the green stalk a tug. "And there haven't been any great storms like the one that hit Gummy Forest in the spring."

"My guess is Mogu," Berry said. She folded

her arms across her chest. "That mischievous troll is always out to steal Candy Fairy treats."

"Maybe," Cocoa said, nodding. A shiver spread to the tip of her wings as she remembered her journey to Black Licorice Swamp with Princess Lolli. When Cocoa's chocolate eggs were missing, she and the fairy princess journeyed to Mogu's cave to get them back. It was a dangerous trek, and Cocoa didn't want to think about going back to that black swamp again.

"I'm thinking it was the Chuchies," Melli said, sitting down on the ground. She leaned against one of the stalks. "You see the ground here? There weren't mounds of brown sugar here yesterday. And Chuchies are short, so it makes sense that they'd try to pull the stalks."

"And Chuchies always leave a mess behind," Berry said, agreeing with Melli.

"Those furry little creatures could have tramped through here last night," Raina said, looking around. "They are so sneaky, they could have come in without anyone seeing them."

"But you know those Chuchies don't act alone," Cocoa added.

"Mogu," Berry said again. "I just know he is behind this."

Melli put her head in her hands. "So what do we do about it?"

"First we need to make sure it really was the Chuchies," Raina said. "Maybe it was someone else?"

The fairy friends were silent as they all considered who might have been responsible.

"What if all the candy is gone tomorrow?" Dash said in a panic.

"Then the Sugar Pops probably won't come," Melli said sadly.

"The Sugar Pops?" Berry, Raina, and Dash all said at the same time.

Melli had been so happy to tell her friends about the Sugar Pops coming, but now the news wasn't as exciting. If there were no crops, there wouldn't be a big celebration.

"Cara overheard the Royal Fairies talking at Candy Castle about them coming to perform," Cocoa explained.

"I was so excited to see them," Melli said sadly. "But who knows if they will come if there's no festival."

"Holy peppermint!" Dash exclaimed. "You

mean Chip, Char, and Carob are going to be here? Right here?" She flew straight up in the air.

Cocoa nodded. "That was the plan," she explained.

"We definitely need to solve this candy corn mystery," Berry said.

"You can bet your sugar fruit chews," Cocoa said. "This was the first year we were going to get to stay till midnight!"

"And meet the Sugar Pops," Dash added with a dreamy look in her eye.

"Well, at least there are a few candy clues," Berry noted. "Do you think we can figure this out?"

"We can solve this mystery," Melli said, standing up. "We have to!"

Raina paced up and down. She tapped her

finger on her chin as she thought out loud. "There's a story in the Fairy Code Book about Lupa the Sugar Fairy," she began. "She was sure that a troll was stealing her sugar fruit chews and wanted to protect her candy."

"Oh, I know that story!" Berry exclaimed. "Lupa caught the troll in the middle of the night and sent him back over the Frosted Mountains. She was very brave."

Melli walked over to Raina. "How did she do that?" she asked.

"Well," Raina said, "the story goes that she built a spy tower so that she could watch the fields at night and spot the troll. She used sticky sugar syrup in a hidden trap to slow the troll down. And she captured him!"

"Wow!" Dash cried. *"So mint."*

The more Melli thought about the crops and the festival, the braver she felt. She had to be as clever as Lupa had been. She knew she had to do something to make sure that the Caramel Moon Festival happened this year.

"I have a plan," she declared. "Let's meet back here right before Sun Dip tomorrow. We're going to build a tower just like Lupa. I'm sure whoever did this will be back for more tonight. And we'll be waiting."

Melli's friends all stared at her. The Caramel Fairy seemed very sure of herself. But would they be successful like Lupa had been? How would they stop whoever—or whatever—was trying to ruin Caramel Moon?

CHAPTER

4

Sweet Moonlight

The sun was just about to slip down below the tops of the Frosted Mountains. Melli stood with her four friends at the edge of Candy Corn Fields. A cool breeze blew their wings, but they were all still. They were anxious to hear Melli's plan for building the spy tower.

"We'll build the tower here," Melli said. She

 34

pointed to a clearing in Lollipop Landing. "We'll be able to see all the fields if we make the tower high enough."

Dash opened her bag. "I brought peppermint sticks that glow in the dark," she said. "I thought that would help."

"And I brought some gummy lanterns," Raina said. She held up two lanterns to show her friends. One lantern glowed a deep red light, and the other orange.

Melli smiled. "Thanks," she said.

Cocoa took a box out of her bag. "And I brought a telescope," she said. "It's made out of the finest chocolate with a special sugar glass lens." She held it up to her eye. "Perfect for spying," she added.

"That looks like the kind of telescope that Lupa used," Raina said, taking a closer look.

"Come on," Melli told them. "There isn't much daylight left, and we've got work to do."

"Where's Berry?" Dash asked, looking around.

Raina shrugged. "She said that she had to get something."

"It's not like we're meeting the Sugar Pops tonight," Cocoa said, joking. "But she probably still wanted to change into some special spy outfit for the spying occasion."

Just then Berry came flying up to the group. "I'm here!" she called. "And I have some sticky fruit syrup for the traps," she said. She showed her friends a large bottle of gooey red syrup. "It's what Lupa used, so I thought it would help."

"Thanks, Berry," Melli told her. "I set some traps down in the fields, and the sticky syrup will be perfect."

"But you know," Raina said, "Chuchies can sniff those traps out. They can pick up scents from miles away."

Melli nodded. "I know," she said, "but it's worth a try. If the thieves aren't the Chuchies, then maybe the traps will stop them."

Quickly the five friends worked together to build a spy tower. Raina and Berry flew in tall lollipop sticks, and Dash and Cocoa lifted rolls of fruit leather to make the floor. Melli tied the lollipop sticks together with licorice vines and secured the tall tower. Then the fairies set up the lanterns and peppermint sticks at the top.

By the time they finished with the tower, the sky was getting dark. There was a chill in the air and Melli shivered.

"Okay, so we'll take turns using Cocoa's telescope," she said. "And we'll check on the traps every hour."

"When we catch the candy corn thieves," Cocoa said, "we'll be the heroes of Caramel Moon!"

"I hope you're right," Melli told her. She picked up the telescope and peered through the lens. "So far the fields are quiet."

Berry wrapped herself in a white shawl. "It's cold out tonight!" she exclaimed.

"Is that new?" Dash asked, admiring Berry's shawl.

"Yes," Berry said proudly. "It's made from

the finest white cotton candy and finished with a raw sugar fringe."

"Wow," Dash said, admiring the details.

"It's warm, too," Berry told her. "Do you want to share it with me?"

Dash shook her head. "No, I like this cold weather," she answered. "It makes me feel like winter is almost here."

"Don't say that!" Raina cried. "We haven't even celebrated Caramel Moon. Winter is a long time away."

"It can't come soon enough," Dash replied. "I want to hit the slopes with my new sled."

Dash lived for the winter, when she could sled. Even though she was the smallest fairy in Sugar Valley, she was a champion on the slopes.

The five friends huddled together as they

watched the fields from the high tower.

Melli stood up and walked to the edge of the tower. She didn't see anything unusual. The Candy Corn stalks all stood upright, swaying in the night breeze. She sighed heavily. "What will we do if we don't see anything?" she asked.

"We just have to be patient," Raina advised. "Lupa had to sit in her tower for a week before she saw anything."

"Raina!" Melli cried out. "We don't have a week! Caramel Moon is tomorrow night!"

The evening wind gently shook the tower.

"It's spooky here," Dash said.

"And dark," Cocoa added. "It's a good thing the moon is almost full so we can keep watch."

"But it is a little scary," Berry said, pulling her knees up to her chest.

"I'll crack another peppermint stick," Dash told them. A little spark from the stick lit up the tower.

Raina yawned. "I'm so sleepy," she said. "I had to clean up Gummy Forest today. Those gummy cubs made a huge mess playing in the woods."

"Maybe we should take turns keeping watch over the fields," Cocoa suggested.

Melli pressed the telescope to her eye. "I'll take the first turn," she said. "I am too nervous to sleep. If something is going to happen, I want to be ready."

"Well, wake us up if you see something," Berry said, lying down. Her eyes were heavy and she longed to get a little rest.

"I'll stay up with you," Cocoa told Melli. "Don't worry," she whispered, "I'm sure we'll see something soon."

Melli hoped Cocoa was right. She kept her eyes on the fields below, searching for any sign. But so far only the winds were making the stalks sway in the moonlight.

5

Super-Spies

The round moon rose high in the sky. Melli was thankful for the soft white moonlight. She kept a careful watch on the fields as her friends slept.

Melli spread Berry's soft white shawl over the sleeping fairies. They were all huddled together on the floor of the tower. Even Cocoa had drifted off to sleep. But Melli was wide awake. She knew that whoever—or whatever—was harming the crops would strike soon. And she wanted to be ready.

She picked up the chocolate telescope and gazed through the lens. Zooming in on the fields below, she looked for any sign of trouble. But the fields were quiet. She would just have to wait.

Melli turned back to her sleeping friends. She was so thankful that they were with her on this spying mission.

Next to Raina, Melli saw the book with the Lupa the Sugar Fairy story. She picked it up and searched for the tale about Lupa and the mischievous troll. As she read about Lupa's adventures, she grew more and more impatient waiting for something to happen in the fields.

Once again she stood up and looked through the telescope.

"Hot caramel!" she cried.

Cocoa woke with a start. "What? What happened?" she said, jumping up.

Melli gave Cocoa the telescope and pointed to the north side of the field.

"Over there!" she said. "I knew it! I knew those little furry Chuchies were the cause of all this mess."

"Look at them," Cocoa said. She watched the Chuchies scurry around on their thin, short legs. "They are so sneaky. Look how they are coming up from underneath the stalks."

"That's why the stalks seem shorter!" Melli declared. "The Chuchies have been digging tunnels in the field to pull the stalks down! They couldn't reach the candy unless they pulled the stalks lower."

"Chocolate sprinkles!" Cocoa exclaimed. "You're right!"

"I'm going to go see exactly what they are doing," Melli said bravely.

Cocoa put the telescope down. "Then I'm going with you." She grabbed Melli's hand. "You shouldn't go alone."

Together, the two fairies flew down into Candy Corn Fields. Melli tried not to think about the long shadows in the field or the howling wind. She flew quickly and landed behind a large candy corn stalk. Without saying a word, she pointed to a mound of brown sugar. Then she and Cocoa hid as a couple of Chuchies shuffled by.

"Meeee, meeeee!" squealed one of the Chuchies. With a little jump, the furry creature grabbed a bunch of candy corn. Then it jumped over the sticky syrup trap.

Another Chuchie popped up from the underground tunnel. It shook off the brown sugar dirt from its pom-pom-shaped body. "Meeee Meeeee!" it sang out. The Chuchie held up a basket and plunked in several pieces of candy corn.

Melli wanted to run out from her hiding space and grab the candy back. She saw about five more Chuchies crawl out of the tunnel with baskets. If she and her friends didn't act soon, all the candy corn would be gone by the time the sun rose. Melli knew that in order to save the crops, she had to be smart. The Chuchies

weren't the cleverest creatures, but they were determined . . . especially about stealing candy.

Waving her hand, she motioned for Cocoa to fly back to the tower, where they could talk.

When they were away from the field, Melli let out a sigh. "How can we stop them? Those mischievous Chuchies can't just take our candy."

Raina stretched and yawned. "Did you see something?" she asked, half asleep. "What's going on?"

As Raina sat up, Berry and Dash opened their eyes. Melli sat down on the floor next to her friends. "Cocoa and I saw the Chuchies taking the candy corn," she told them. "They dug tunnels under the fields."

"We have to stop them!" Dash exclaimed.

"But how?" Raina asked. "Chuchies are quick, and strong."

"But not always smart," Berry pointed out.

Melli gazed toward the field. "We need a plan," she said. She bent down and picked up Raina's book.

"What would Lupa do?" Dash asked. "She caught the troll. She knew what she was doing."

"She was one of the bravest Candy Fairies ever," Raina said. "She defeated lots of trolls and dragons."

Berry stood up. "We can be just as clever," she said. "No way are those little Chuchies going to get away with stealing candy corn . . . or ruining the Caramel Moon Festival."

"Or spoiling our chance to meet the Sugar Pops," Cocoa chimed in.

Hugging the book to her chest, Melli wished she could be as brave and as clever as Lupa had been. She stared at the Chuchies scurrying around in the moonlit field. "We have to do something to make them stop."

Raina stood up and put her arm around Melli. "There's still time," she said calmly.

"There's a ton of candy corn this year," Cocoa added. "There will be plenty for the celebration."

Berry shook her head. "But Melli's right. We need a plan. We need a way to stop the Chuchies. If we don't, we can say good-bye to the Sugar Pops."

"Don't be so sour," Raina said. "We can come up with a plan."

"But we better act fast," Melli said, biting her

nails. "The Chuchies have almost cleared the north part of the field."

She wanted to believe that she and her friends could stop what was going on . . . the only question was how!

CHAPTER
6

Ghoulish Plans

As Melli and her friends huddled together in the tower, a strong wind blew through the fields. The wind picked up Berry's white shawl and blew it off the tower into the dark night.

"Oh no!" Berry cried. She leaned over the side of the tower. "That's my new shawl!" She squinted into the darkness. "Where did it go?"

Dash got up and stood next to Berry. Leaning over the railing, she searched down below.

"We'll find it," Raina said gently. "Don't worry."

"I see the shawl," Dash said. She pointed to the left of the tower. "There it is!"

"Oh, thank you, Dash," Berry gushed, giving her tiny friend a tight squeeze.

"It looks like a ghost, doesn't it?" Cocoa said, looking down at the shawl.

Raina shivered. "Don't talk about ghosts," she said. "It's creepy enough out here in the moonlight and howling winds."

Dash put her hands on her hips. "Oh, come on," she said. "Are you really scared?"

Melli's eyes grew wide. "That's it!" she exclaimed. "Raina, you're brilliant!"

Berry, Raina, Dash, and Cocoa all shared confused looks.

"That's the perfect way to stop the Chuchies," Melli declared, grinning.

"What are you talking about?" Cocoa asked. "Did I just miss something?"

Melli couldn't help smiling. She knew that her plan was going to work. Swooping down to the ground, she picked up Berry's shawl and brought it back up to the tower. She put the shawl over her head and reached her hands out to the sides.

"Put the candy corn down!" she said in the spookiest voice she could.

Cocoa laughed out loud.

But Dash clapped. "Scare the Chuchies!" she said. She flapped her wings and flew up in the air. "Oh, that is pure sugar!"

"Do you think that will work?" Berry asked. She took the shawl off Melli's head and hugged it close. "This is made from the finest sugar, you know."

Cocoa rolled her eyes. "Yes, we know," she said.

"It's a good idea," Raina told Melli. "Chuchies are known to react out of fear." She opened her Fairy Code Book and flipped through the pages. Then she ran her finger down the page until she found what she was looking for at the bottom. "Chuchies react quickly to things that confuse or scare them," she read.

"If it's written in the Fairy Code Book, then it must be true!" Melli said happily.

Raina grinned, but Berry shook her head.

"Come on," Berry said. "How are you going to get those Chuchies to believe that my shawl is a ghost?"

Cocoa saw Melli starting to panic.

"We'll figure out a way," Cocoa said. "We can do it!"

Melli was thankful for Cocoa's enthusiasm. She held up a large round lollipop. "We can drape the shawl over this," she explained. "And then we can put the stick in the ground." She tilted her head and examined the ghost. "Our ghost is going to need some kind of eerie glow."

"Use one of my peppermint sticks," Dash suggested. She flew closer to Melli and cracked open one of her glow-in-the-dark candies. Sprinkling the peppermint candy around the inside of the shawl made their ghost start to glow.

"Hey, now it's starting to look like the Ghost of Candy Corn Fields!" Cocoa cheered.

Raina looked up from her book. "The ghost will need a voice," she said.

"I know!" Cocoa cried. "Wait one second!" She flew off the tower and out into the darkness. In a flash she was back with a chocolate sugar cone. She broke off the pointy end. "Here, talk into this," she told Melli. "This cone from Chocolate Woods will make you sound bigger and scarier."

"Thanks, Cocoa," Melli said, taking the cone. She did as Cocoa had told her and spoke into the long sugar cone.

"Put down the candy corn!" Melli bellowed.

 61

"It still sounds like you," Berry said. She crossed her arms over her chest.

"Berry!" Cocoa cried. "Maybe your sugar clips are in too tight." She pointed to the sugarcoated fruit chews in Berry's hair.

Berry ignored Cocoa. Tapping her finger on her chin, Berry thought for a moment. "Hold on," she said. "I have an idea." She dove off the top of the tower again. "I'll be right back."

"What is she up to?" Melli asked Raina.

Raina shrugged. "You never know with Berry," she said.

Berry appeared with a piece of fruit leather and spread it over the cone's wide opening. "Okay," she said. "Melli, now try and talk," she instructed.

This time when Melli spoke, her voice came

through the cone muffled and distant. She really did sound like a ghost!

"Berry!" Melli cried. "You did it! What a great idea."

"*Ghoul* work," Cocoa told her, laughing at her own joke.

Berry grinned. "Never hurts to have a little fruit around," she said.

Dash picked up the telescope. "We'd better get down to the fields fast," she said. "Those Chuchies are working quickly."

"So it's okay if we use your shawl?" Melli asked Berry.

"Yes," Berry said. "Licking lollipops! This might work!"

The five fairies grabbed the supplies and headed down to the fields. In the dim light they worked to make the ghost stand up and loom over the fields. They pushed the lollipop stick deep into the ground. Then they tied another stick across, making a T shape so the ghost would appear to have two arms.

Melli stood back and admired their ghost.

"The ghost needs eyes," Cocoa whispered. "He has to see what the Chuchies are doing!"

"Hold on," Dash said. "I think I have two more peppermints. A ghost should have glowing eyes, don't you think?" From her pocket Dash took out her last two candies and stuck them onto the shawl. The bright green mints looked like glowing, ghoulish eyes.

"Hot caramel!" Melli said very quietly. "I think we've got a ghost! Let's move this ghost closer to the Chuchies."

Now all they had to do was convince the Chuchies that there was a ghost haunting Candy Corn Fields.

CHAPTER 7

Ghost Lessons

Together, the five fairies were flying down to the north side of Candy Corn Fields. Each of them held on to the lollipop stick that formed the body of the ghost. They zoomed quickly through the air, heading down to begin their plan to save Caramel Moon.

"Now this really looks real," Dash said. She

glanced over her shoulder. "Doesn't this look like a flying ghost?"

"Shhh," Cocoa shushed her. "We don't want the Chuchies to hear us. We have to set up first." She pointed to the bunch of Chuchies gathering up the candy corn. They were so focused on their task that they didn't even look up.

"Oh, I hope this works," Melli whispered. She kept her eyes focused on the fields below. Her heart ached as she noticed all the dirt mounds that the Chuchies had made by digging tunnels.

What a gooey mess, she thought.

"Everything is going to be okay," Cocoa said. She knew from Melli's expression that she was worried. "We'll get the Chuchies out of here and still save the crops in time for Caramel Moon."

More than anything, Melli wanted to believe her best friend. But she wasn't one hundred percent sure the plan would work. Chuchies were known to be mischievous, but would they scare so easily? Would they listen?

The friends landed on the soft brown sugar ground. They huddled behind a lush green stalk and found a good spot for the ghost.

"On the count of three," Cocoa said, "let's lift the ghost up and stick it into the ground."

"One, two, three," Berry counted.

The fairies heaved the ghost up and secured the stick in the ground.

Standing back, Berry grinned. "Sure as sugar, this looks like a spooky ghost to me!" she said in a hushed voice.

"Let's hide over here," Raina suggested. She

pointed behind a stalk. "We'll be able to see, but we'll be well hidden. Melli, do you have the sugar cone?"

"I do," Melli said. She took the cone from her bag. Then she took a deep breath. "Here I go...." She held the cone with the end wrapped in fruit leather. In her loudest, deepest voice, she called, "Who is there?"

Peeking out from their hiding places, the fairies watched the Chuchies freeze.

"Meee, meee, meee?" a Chuchie sang out, shaking.

A few Chuchies put down their baskets and turned around. They seemed panicked. And then they noticed the ghost.

"Who is stealing my candy?" Melli said

into the cone. She peeked around the stalk to see what the Chuchies were doing.

"Keep talking," Raina whispered. "You've got their attention!"

"I am the Ghost of Candy Corn Fields," Melli said. "These candies are for the Caramel Moon Festival."

A few more Chuchies gathered around. All the hairs on their pom-pom bodies were standing up straight!

They are listening, Melli thought. *The plan is working!*

"You are not allowed to take this candy!" Melli continued. "The candy here is for sharing, not for stealing."

"Meeeeeeeeeeee!" a chorus of Chuchies cried.

Dash put her hand to her mouth to quiet

her giggles. She couldn't believe the Chuchies believed their lollipop ghost was real.

Cocoa gave her a stern look, reminding her to be serious.

Raina squeezed Dash's hand. And the four of them kept careful watch.

"They're leaving!" Raina whispered. "Look!"

Melli put down the cone and saw that Raina was right. The Chuchies were crawling back into their tunnels.

"Let's keep the ghost up here in the field," Raina suggested, "just to be sure that the Chuchies don't come back."

"I don't think they're coming back," Berry said as she watched the furry little creatures scurry back into their holes.

"Maybe Mogu didn't put them up to this?"

Cocoa asked. The Chuchies lived in the Black Licorice Swamp, where only pretzels grew along the banks of the dark, salty shores. The Chuchies craved sweet treats and often tried to get Candy Fairy candy.

"If Mogu was behind all this, he won't be pleased," Raina said. "But from what I've read about Chuchies, they won't be back here. They were definitely spooked."

"Sure as sugar," Melli said with a grin. She hugged her friends. "We got the Chuchies to leave!" She fluttered her wings and flew up in the air.

"I had no doubt," Berry said, folding her arms across her chest.

Before Cocoa could respond, Melli flew back down to her friends.

"The fields look terrible!" Melli cried. "The tunnels the Chuchies dug have ruined the ground."

Dash shot up in the air and checked out the area. "Wow, those Chuchies sure were fast."

"And messy," Raina said, joining Dash in the air. "They only ate the top parts of the candy corn and left the yellow-and-orange parts on the ground." She shook her head. "We need a clean-up plan."

"And soon," Berry added. She shot up in the air next to her friends. "Caramel Moon is tomorrow night!"

Melli knew her friends were right. Scaring the Chuchies away was only the beginning. There was more work to be done to prepare for the festival.

Gazing up at the lollipop ghost, Melli was thankful the Chuchies were gone. "Good job," she said. "Thank you, Ghost of Candy Corn Fields."

Berry smiled. "Wearing my new shawl, it's definitely the best-dressed ghost," she said, laughing.

"Don't worry, Berry," Melli told her. "I'll make sure to get this back to you before Caramel Moon."

Thinking of Caramel Moon made Melli a little nervous. Could she and her friends get the fields cleaned up before the full moon?

8

Clean-up Crew

The first light of morning peeked through the clouds high above the Frosted Mountains. Melli squinted up at the rising sun.

"Come on," she called to her friends. "We must finish cleaning up the fields before daylight."

Even though she was tired, Melli kept on

working. She reached for a few pieces of candy corn on the ground and put them in her basket. She had already collected a mound of half-eaten candy corn, but there were still yellow-and-orange pieces of candy scattered.

Since the Chuchies had left the fields, she and her friends had been picking up all the half-eaten candies. Still, the fields were a mess. The mounds of dirt from the Chuchies' tunnels made Candy Corn Fields a difficult maze to manage. Normally, all the fairies danced around the stalks as they picked the candy. And this year with the Sugar Pops playing, there'd be more dancing than ever before.

Where will everyone dance? Melli wondered.

She thought back to when her sister had told her about the Sugar Pops coming to the festival.

She had been so excited and had imagined dancing all night under the Caramel Moon. Now those thoughts were buried—there'd be no dancing tonight. The Sugar Pops would probably not want to come.

Then a terribly sour thought popped into her head.

What if the festival is canceled?

"Ready?" Cocoa asked, grabbing a handle of the basket. She looked over at Melli.

When Melli didn't answer, Cocoa snapped her fingers in front of her friend's face. "Melli!" she said. "Are you listening?"

Cocoa's voice brought Melli out of her thoughts.

"Sorry," she said. "I'm ready now."

Melli threw two more pieces into the overflowing basket. Then she lifted up her end of the basket and flapped her wings with all her might. The basket was heavy. "Those Chuchies took more of the crops than I had thought," Melli said, sighing. "And they wasted so many of the candies. Look at all these half-eaten pieces!"

The two fairies flew to the edge of the field and dumped the basket.

Melli wiped her hand on her forehead. "I'm not sure those stalks on the north side are ready to harvest," she said to Cocoa. "The tunnels dug up part of the crops there. I'm afraid this prank that the Chuchies played is going to affect the festival."

"You worry too much," Berry said, flying up behind her. "I think we all need to rest."

Raina and Dash dumped their basket of

ruined candy corn onto the pile. "We've been working all night," Raina added.

"Rest?" Melli cried. "How can I rest? Look at this field."

Cocoa took out a piece of chocolate bark from her bag. "Everyone calm down," she said. "Let's take a break and think about our next move."

"You have any more chocolate bark?" Dash asked, licking her lips. She was always hungry, and seeing Cocoa with that chocolate made her even hungrier. Dash might have been tiny, but her appetite wasn't! "I think better on a full stomach," she added.

"Here you go, Dash." Cocoa smiled as she handed Dash a piece of chocolate. When Cocoa offered a piece to Melli, she shook her head. She wasn't hungry. "What am I going to tell Princess

Lolli?" she asked. Even though the gentle fairy ruled over Candy Kingdom with a sweet and truthful touch, Melli was nervous. She didn't want to disappoint her.

"Tell me what?" a sweet voice asked.

The five fairies looked up and saw the beautiful fairy princess hovering above them.

"Good morning," Princess Lolli said as she flew down beside the fairies. Her strawberry-blond hair fell loosely around her shoulders, and her candy-jeweled crown sparkled in the morning light. "You look as if you've been up all night!" she exclaimed.

"We have been," Melli told the ruling princess. She bowed her head. "We've been trying to clean up the mess."

Princess Lolli looked around the fields. "The

Chuchies have been here, haven't they?" she said. "I can spot their messy work. Those creatures are slow to learn." She shook her head. "Their greed always gets them into trouble."

"We taught them a lesson!" Dash blurted out.

Raising her eyebrows, Princess Lolli said, "Tell me what happened."

As Melli told the princess the story of the Chuchies and the Ghost of Candy Corn Fields, Princess Lolli nodded.

"I see," the fairy princess said at the end of Melli's tale. "While scaring someone isn't very nice, teaching them that there are consequences to stealing is an important and valuable lesson."

"But what about Caramel Moon?" Melli asked. Her wings twitched. She was so nervous about what Princess Lolli would say.

"Is it true that the Sugar Pops are coming?" Berry asked.

Princess Lolli grinned. "Yes, the Sugar Pops are coming to play tonight," she told the fairies. "Your clean-up crew has done good work, but I'm afraid we've got lots to do before the festival." She took a small pouch from her bag. "Here is some magic sugar dust," she said. "I think this will help the crops on the north side. After such an invasion, the crops need to feel secure to sweeten fully."

"How can we help?" Melli asked. "We want to make sure that the festival happens this year. And that all the Candy Fairies can enjoy the candy corn."

"There is something that you can do," Princess Lolli said. Her silver wings fluttered. "Are you willing?"

Melli and her friends all nodded. They were eager to do whatever the fairy princess told them. The thought of not having a Caramel Moon Festival was too bitter to consider.

9

Sugar Dust

Do you really think this will work?" Melli asked Raina. While the others were still collecting the ruined candies, Melli pulled Raina aside. "Have you ever read anything about this magic sugar dust that Princess Lolli gave us?"

"I haven't," Raina admitted. She shook her head slowly. She wished she could have told

Melli a story about a time when sugar dust saved a candy corn crop, but she knew of no such tale.

Melli's wings drooped. "Oh." She sighed sadly.

"Remember all those stories about Lupa," Raina told her. "You have to keep up hope. Lupa always saved the day."

"But I'm not Lupa," Melli said, bowing her head. She turned and saw the ghost still standing in the fields. In the morning light the ghost didn't look as real. The moonlight had helped to create a spooky glow.

"You taught the Chuchies a lesson," Raina reminded her. "You were very clever, and I'm sure the ghost will protect the fields."

The fairies all gathered around Melli. They didn't like to see her so sad.

Cocoa was the first to speak. "Princess Lolli

gave you a task," she said, trying to snap her friend out of her sour state.

Knowing that Cocoa was right, Melli looked down at the pouch of sugar dust.

"Anything Princess Lolli gives is touched with some kind of magic," Raina said kindly. "The first thing you must do is sprinkle the crops."

Melli knew she was right. She hugged her friends and flew to the north side of the fields. Carefully, she spread the fine sugar dust over the crops below. She hoped the sugar dust worked quickly—there wasn't much time!

Just as Princess Lolli had instructed, she tried to think only good thoughts as she threw the fine sugar. She imagined all the fairies in the kingdom picking candy corn, and the sweet smells that would fill the air. She pushed any sour thoughts out of her head and started to hum "Yum Pop." Thinking of her favorite band sweetened her thoughts and made her smile.

When Melli had finished her task, she went back to the spy tower. Her friends had started to take it down.

"We should build another one of these," Dash said. She untied a licorice vine, and two lollipops fell down. "This was fun."

"No thanks," Berry said. "I was freezing all night. I much prefer to sleep inside."

Cocoa saw that Melli was back. "How'd it go?" she asked.

"I did what Princess Lolli told me to do," Melli said to her friends. "I kept thinking of all the fun we'd have tonight."

"*Choc-o-rific!*" Cocoa exclaimed. "If that's what

you were thinking, then the crops will be extra sweet."

"That's for sure," Berry added. "We're going to have a great time tonight. Especially when the Sugar Pops play!" She touched her hand to her colorful fruit-chew clips. "I made some new fruit jewels for the occasion. I want to sparkle so the Sugar Pops notice me."

Dash rolled her eyes. "I don't think they care about fruit jewels," she told her. "They are very focused on their music."

"It says in *Sugar Beats* that the band loves to entertain," Raina said. All her friends looked at her with wide eyes. "What?" she said. "I read *Sugar Beats* too! There's lots of good information in that magazine."

For the first time since Melli had seen the

Chuchies in the fields, she laughed. It felt good to joke around and be with her friends.

"There's one more thing that Princess Lolli told us to do," Melli said. "Are you all ready?"

The four fairies stood in front of Melli, nodding. "We're ready," they all said together.

They flew down to the edge of the fields to the north side, where the stalks were sunk into the ground.

"Okay," Melli said. "On the count of three, we'll give these stalks a pull."

"Remember to think sweet thoughts!" Raina reminded them.

A cool breeze moved their wings, but the fairies didn't budge from their spots. With their eyes shut tight, each one thought of a sweet memory as she pulled a green stalk up. Each of their thoughts included a time when the friends were all together, and soon the stalks reached their full height.

Melli felt a tingling in her wings and opened her eyes. "I think we might have done it," she said. "At least, I hope so."

"There are a few more stalks to pull," Cocoa said. "We better hurry."

The fairies worked to pull the stalks up, and they kept thinking only sweet thoughts.

"I guess we won't know how the candy tastes until tonight," Dash said. "But I think the fields look much better than earlier today."

"Sure as sugar," Raina said. "Don't worry, Melli. I truly believe this will be one of the best Caramel Moon Festivals ever."

Melli wished with all her heart that her friends

94

were right. She hoped that Princess Lolli's sugar dust and her friends' sweet thoughts were strong enough to heal the fields. She wouldn't know for sure until that night, when the Caramel Moon rose high in the sky. . . . And she couldn't wait!

10

Under the Caramel Moon

Melli sat at the top of a caramel tree with Cocoa. As they waited for the first stars of the evening sky to appear, Melli bit her nails. She was so nervous!

"I can't believe tonight is Caramel Moon," Cocoa said. She was swinging her legs back and forth. "I'm so excited to see the Sugar Pops—and eat all that candy corn."

"I know," Melli said. "I've been looking forward to this for so long." She looked down at her bitten nails. "But then the whole Chuchies thing happened."

"But we solved that problem," Cocoa said. "With a little *spooktacular* show."

Melli laughed. "We did, didn't we?" she said. "Let's just hope the crops will be ready by midnight."

"You worry too much," Cocoa told her. "Come on, let's get going. I want a good spot. It's not every day that we get to hear the Sugar Pops!"

"You mean *see* the Sugar Pops!" Melli said, correcting her. "Do you think Char will be wearing his sprinkle hat? I'll just melt if he is!"

They flew over Caramel Hills toward Candy Corn Fields, and Melli held her breath as the moon came into view. The large moon looked like a golden caramel circle in the sky. Seeing the round, full moon rise made Melli fly faster. She couldn't wait to get to the fields. The crisp air sent a shiver down her wings, and she breathed in the sweet scent of ripe candy corn.

"Melli!" Cara called. "Wait up!" The little fairy flew up to her big sister. "I have never seen such a beautiful moonrise. And look at all those fairies!" She pointed down below to the large crowd of fairies flocking to the field. Word that the Sugar Pops were playing had spread far and wide. "Melli, thank you for getting me permission to come."

"You bet," Melli said. She gave her little sister

a hug. Princess Lolli had said it was her pleasure to give Cara permission—especially after all the work Melli had done to save the crops.

"Melli! Cocoa!"

Raina and Dash were waving at their friends. They were standing in front of the stage set up on the north side of the fields.

"We got here early," Raina said as her friends landed beside her.

"But so did everyone else!" Dash added.

Melli looked around. The stalks had returned to their normal height, and there seemed to be plenty of candy corn on the stems. "Everything looks great," she said, amazed.

"They don't call Princess Lolli the ruling fairy princess for nothing," Cocoa chimed in. "I told you that you worry too much."

Melli reached down and plucked a ripe candy corn. She took a bite and her wings flapped with excitement. "Hot caramel!" she exclaimed. "This is the most delicious candy corn ever!"

Each of her friends took a bite and smiled.

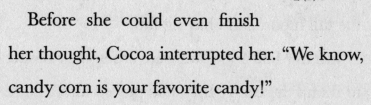

"We did it!" Dash said. She reached for more of the colorful candy. "These are my favorite—"

Before she could even finish her thought, Cocoa interrupted her. "We know, candy corn is your favorite candy!"

The friends all laughed. Every candy Dash tasted was her favorite candy!

"Hello, fairies!" Berry cried as she swooped down next to her friends. She was wearing a new dress with brightly colored fruit chews in her hair. She looked beautiful.

"I see you're all ready to meet the Sugar Pops," Cocoa said, eyeing her fancy friend.

"Oh, I can't wait!" Berry exclaimed.

"First we need to pick the candy," Melli said. "After all, that is what this night is all about."

Around them, fairies of all kinds were busy collecting candy corn in large baskets. The fairies were working hard in the bright light of the full moon. And having fun.

Just as Melli and Cara were lifting their basket to dump the candy they had picked into a large barrel, Cara froze.

"Sweet sugar!" Cara screamed. Her dark eyes were focused straight ahead. She couldn't say anything—she could only point.

Following Cara's gaze, Melli saw what had made her sister scream. There on the stage were the Sugar Pops! Chip, Char, and Carob were tuning their gummy guitars.

"Carob's wearing his sprinkle hat." Melli sighed. "He is so sweet!"

As the Sugar Pops started to play, more fairies moved closer to the stage. The music filled the night as all the fairies rejoiced.

Melli stood with her friends close to the stage, listening to the Sugar Pops play.

Princess Lolli appeared on the stage. Her bright pink dress glowed in the moonlight. She greeted the crowd of fairies with a huge smile. "Welcome to the Caramel Moon Festival," she said.

There was a huge roar of applause.

"I am so happy to report that this year's crop was saved by Melli and her friends," the princess said. "We had an unfortunate disturbance, but these fairies came to the rescue. We owe them a huge fairy cheer, and our deepest gratitude."

Melli blushed. She hadn't thought that Princess Lolli would thank them in front of everyone—including the Sugar Pops.

She felt Cara's elbow push her side. "Look," Cara said, pointing to the stage. "You have to go up there! You deserve it. You saved the crops!"

Melli grabbed her friends' hands, and all of them flew up onstage.

"Let's hear it for these fairies," Carob sang out. He turned to Melli. "Do you have a special song request?"

Melli was so overwhelmed that she couldn't

speak! Carob was inches away from her—and his chocolate brown eyes were looking directly at her!

"'Yum Pop' is her favorite song," Cocoa said, coming to her rescue.

"We know that one," Carob teased. He strummed the first chord on his bright red gummy guitar.

Sweet sugar! Melli thought as she swayed onstage to her favorite tune. She was thankful for the Ghost of Candy Corn Fields, and her good friends. All around her, fairies were smiling and singing along with the Sugar Pops.

Lupa would be proud, she thought.

This was a night that would be recorded in the Fairy Code Book. The Caramel Moon Festival was always a supersweet time, but this year had been different. She turned to her friends, and together they all sang "Yum Pop" with Chip, Char, and Carob. The moment was as sweet as the candy corn they had picked.

FIND OUT

WHAT HAPPENS IN

Cool Mint

A cool morning breeze blew through Marshmallow Marsh. Dash, the smallest Mint Fairy in Sugar Valley, was very excited. She had been working on her new sled all year, and now her work was done. Finally the sled was ready to ride. And just in time! Sledding season was about to begin.

Many fairies in Sugar Valley didn't like the cool months as much as Dash. Each season in Sugar Valley had its own special flavors and candies— and Dash loved them all. She was a small fairy with a large appetite!

Dash was happiest during the winter. All the mint candies were grown in the chilly air that swept through the valley during the wintertime. She enjoyed the refreshing mint scents and the clean white powdered sugar. But for her, the thrill of competing was the sweetest part of the season. She had waited all year for this chance to try out her new sled!

The Marshmallow Run was one of the brightest highlights of the winter for Dash. The sled race was one of the most competitive and challenging races in Sugar Valley. And for the past two years, Dash had won first place. But this year was different. This year Dash wanted to be the fastest fairy in the kingdom—and set a new speed record. No fairy had been able to beat Pep the Mint Fairy's record in years. He had stopped racing now and was one of Princess Lolli's closest advisers. But no one had come close to breaking his record.

Dash had carefully picked the finest candy to make her sled the fastest. While many of her fairy friends had been playing in the fields, she had been hard at work. She was sure that the slick red licorice blades with iced tips and the cool peppermint seat was going to make her new sled ride perfectly. If she was going to break the record this year, she'd need all the help she could get.

Dash looked around. No one else was on the

slopes at this early hour. She took a deep breath. The conditions were perfect for her test run. "Here I go," she said.

On her new sled Dash glided down the powdered sugar trail that led into the white marshmallow peaks. It was a tricky and sticky course, but Dash had done the run so many times she knew every turn and dip of the lower part of the Frosted Mountains. She steered her sled easily and sped down the mountain. The iced tips on the sled's blades made all the difference! She was picking up great speed as she neared the bottom of the slope.

When she reached the finish line, she checked her watch. Had she done it? Had she beat the Candy Kingdom record?

"Holy peppermint!" she cried.

Dash couldn't believe how close she was to beating her best time. She had to shave off a few more seconds to break the record, but this was the fastest run she had ever had. Dash grinned. *This year is my year*, she thought happily.

Suddenly a sugar fly landed on her shoulder with a note. Dash recognized the neat handwriting of her friend Raina. Raina was a Gummy Fairy and always followed the rules of the Fairy Code Book. She was a gentle and kind fairy who was also a very good friend.

"Raina told you that you'd find me here, huh?" Dash said to the small fly.

The tiny messenger nodded.

Dash opened Raina's note. "She thinks she has to remind me about Sun Dip," Dash said to the fly. She shook her head, smiling.

Sun Dip was a time when all the fairies came together to talk about their day and share their candy. Dash loved the large feast of the day and enjoyed sharing treats with her friends. Now that the weather was turning colder, her mint candies were all coming up from the ground. Peppermint Grove was sprouting peppermint sticks and mint suckers for the winter season.

Dash looked up and saw the sun was still high above the top of the mountains. She had time for a couple more runs. She was so close to beating the record. How could she stop now?

"Tell Raina that I'll be there as soon as I can," Dash told the sugar fly. The tiny fly nodded. Then he flew off toward Gummy Forest to deliver the message.

Flapping her wings, Dash flew back to the top of the slope with her new sled. She had to keep practicing.

My friends will understand, she thought.

As she reached the top of the slope, Dash could only think about one thing. Wouldn't all the fairies be surprised when the smallest Mint Fairy beat the record? Dash couldn't wait to see their faces! And to get the first-place prize! The sweet success of winning the Marshmallow Run was a large chocolate marshmallow trophy. It was truly a delicious way to mark the sweet victory of winning the race.

With those happy, sweet thoughts in her head, Dash took off. The rush of wind on her face felt great as she picked up speed down the mountain. A few more runs and she'd beat the record, sure as sugar.

This year everyone would be talking about Dash—the fastest Mint Fairy ever!